ANN M. MARTIN

THE BABY-SITTERS CLUB®

GOOD-BYE STACEY, GOOD-BYE

A GRAPHIC NOVEL BY

GABRIELA EPSTEIN

WITH COLOR BY BRADEN LAMB

An Imprint of
SCHOLASTIC

Library of Congress Control Number: 2021937393

ISBN 978-1-338-61605-7 (hardcover)
ISBN 978-1-338-61604-0 (paperback)

10 9 8 7 6 5 4 3 2 1   22 23 24 25 26

Printed in China 62
First edition, February 2022

Edited by Cassandra Pelham Fulton and David Levithan
Book design by Shivana Sookdeo
Creative Director: Phil Falco
Publisher: David Saylor

With love to Peanut Butter
from Jelly

A. M. M.

To the Menapace family,
No matter what city you're in, you have always
made your house a home to me. Thank you.

G. E.

KRISTY THOMAS
PRESIDENT

CLAUDIA KISHI
VICE PRESIDENT

STACEY MCGILL
TREASURER

MARY ANNE SPIER
SECRETARY

DAWN SCHAFER
ALTERNATE OFFICER

JESSI RAMSEY
JUNIOR OFFICER

MALLORY PIKE
JUNIOR OFFICER

CHAPTER 1

STACEY, GUESS WHAT!

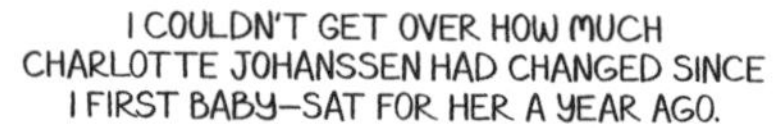
I COULDN'T GET OVER HOW MUCH CHARLOTTE JOHANSSEN HAD CHANGED SINCE I FIRST BABY-SAT FOR HER A YEAR AGO.

WOW. WHOSE HOUSE WILL YOU BE STAYING AT?
IT'S AT VANESSA PIKE'S, AND WE'RE GOING TO THE MOVIES FIRST.
SHE USED TO BE QUIET, A LITTLE SAD, AND WITH NO FRIENDS HER AGE.

NOW SHE WAS HAPPY AND FRIENDLY AND HAD A NEW BEST FRIEND EACH WEEK.
IT'LL BE FOUR OF US. ME, VANESSA, SUKI, AND MERRY.

HELLO!
HER MOM THOUGHT THE CHANGE WAS PARTLY DUE TO CHARLOTTE NOT BEING CHALLENGED ENOUGH AT SCHOOL AND NEEDING TO SKIP A GRADE (WHICH SHE DID)...
MOMMY!

THANKS FOR TODAY. YOU'RE HER FAVORITE SITTER.
AND PARTLY BECAUSE OF ME!
YOU'VE HELPED CHARLOTTE LEARN A LOT ABOUT HERSELF AND ABOUT GETTING ALONG WITH OTHER CHILDREN.
THANK YOU. REALLY, THOUGH, I'M JUST DOING MY JOB!
BYE, CHARLOTTE --
AW, STACEY, DON'T GO!
SORRY, BUDDY. I'LL SEE YOU AGAIN NEXT WEEK!
IT WAS NICE TO BE SOMEBODY'S FAVORITE.

IT WAS ALMOST 5:30, SO I WENT STRAIGHT TO CLAUDIA'S HOUSE FOR A BABY-SITTERS CLUB MEETING.
HI, CLAUD! WHAT'S UP?
THIS IS CLAUDIA KISHI. SHE HAS HER OWN PHONE LINE THAT WE USE FOR BUSINESS. THAT'S WHY SHE'S THE VICE PRESIDENT.
STACEY, YOU WILL NEVER BELIEVE WHAT I JUST HEARD.
WHAT?
HOWIE ASKED DORIANNE TO GO TO THE LIBRARY WITH HIM THIS AFTERNOON.
WHAT? BUT HE ASKED ME TO THE DANCE.
MAYBE THEY'RE DOING A PROJECT TOGETHER OR SOMETHING.
YEAH, THAT MUST BE IT.
CLAUDIA IS ALSO MY VERY BEST FRIEND.

WHATEVER. HOWIE'S A JERK AND MISSING OUT.
YOU SAID IT.
ha ha ha
WE'VE ONLY KNOWN EACH OTHER FOR A LITTLE OVER A YEAR, AND WE'RE AMAZINGLY DIFFERENT.
FOR EXAMPLE, CLAUDIA IS A TERRIBLE STUDENT AND A GREAT ARTIST. I'M A GOOD STUDENT, BUT I DON'T KNOW A THING ABOUT ART.
ILU
B
S
C
ON THE OTHER HAND, CLAUDIA AND I ARE BOTH SORT OF SOPHISTICATED.
AND WE BOTH LOVE TO DRESS IN WILD, FLASHY CLOTHES.
DING-DONG!

HEY, GUYS!
YOU DIDN'T START WITHOUT US, DID YOU?
KRISTY THOMAS IS THE FOUNDER AND PRESIDENT OF THE BSC.
MARY ANNE SPIER IS THE SECRETARY. HER JOB IS TO SCHEDULE BABY-SITTING APPOINTMENTS AND KEEP TRACK OF THE CLUB NOTEBOOK.
DAWN SCHAFER IS OUR ALTERNATE OFFICER. SHE TAKES OVER THE DUTIES OF ANY OTHER CLUB MEMBER WHO CAN'T COME TO A MEETING FOR SOME REASON.
JESSI RAMSEY IS ONE OF OUR JUNIOR OFFICERS. SHE RECENTLY MOVED HERE FROM NEW JERSEY. JUNIOR OFFICERS DON'T WORK AS MANY JOBS OR LATE INTO THE EVENING.

MALLORY PIKE IS OUR OTHER JUNIOR MEMBER. SHE HAS SEVEN SIBLINGS AND A TON OF BABY-SITTING EXPERIENCE.
WE ALSO HAVE TWO ASSOCIATE MEMBERS, LOGAN BRUNO AND SHANNON KILBOURNE. THEY DON'T COME TO MEETINGS. WE JUST PHONE THEM FOR HELP WHEN WE GET TOO BUSY.
AND, FINALLY, THERE'S ME! I'M THE TREASURER AND RESPONSIBLE FOR MANAGING CLUB DUES.

HERE'S HOW IT WORKS: PEOPLE CALL US DURING MEETINGS WHEN THEY NEED SITTERS, AND WE ASSIGN JOBS ACCORDING TO WHO'S FREE.
HELLO? BABY-SITTERS CLUB...
STACEY, YOU'VE GOT CHARLOTTE JOHANSSEN NEXT WEEK.
TODAY WAS A GOOD DAY -- WE EACH GOT ONE JOB.
AND I'D GET TO SEE MY FAVORITE KID AGAIN SOON.

SO...WHAT'S THIS I HEARD ABOUT DORIANNE AND HOWIE?
UGH! DON'T REMIND ME.

SHE'S STILL PROCESSING.
AW, STACE...

RING RING!

A LATE CALL? THE MEETING IS SUPPOSED TO BE OVER.
IT'S A GOOD THING WE'RE STILL HERE.

HELLO, BABY-SITTERS CLUB... OH, HI, MOM.

HONEY, CAN YOU PLEASE COME HOME?
BUT IT'S ONLY FIVE AFTER SIX.

I'D LIKE YOU TO HURRY HOME, PLEASE. IT'S IMPORTANT.
OKAY.
I'LL BE RIGHT THERE.

I HAVE TO GO, GUYS.

I DON'T KNOW WHAT IT IS, BUT SOMETHING'S WRONG.

CHAPTER 2

HERE I AM!
MOM, WHAT'S THE MATTER?

OH, STACE, I'M SORRY. I DIDN'T MEAN TO WORRY YOU.

WE HAVE SOMETHING TO TELL YOU, THAT'S ALL.

HAVE A SEAT. DINNER'S ALMOST READY.

YOU'RE NOT MAKING ME GO TO A NEW DOCTOR, ARE YOU?

I HAVE TYPE I DIABETES.

MY PANCREAS DOESN'T PRODUCE ENOUGH INSULIN, WHICH IT NEEDS TO CONVERT SUGAR TO ENERGY. TO HELP KEEP THINGS IN BALANCE, I GIVE MYSELF INSULIN SHOTS EVERY DAY.

WHEN I WAS FIRST DIAGNOSED, MY PARENTS BECAME REALLY OVERPROTECTIVE AND TOOK ME TO A LOT OF DIFFERENT DOCTORS.
IT DROVE ME BANANAS. THINGS CALMED DOWN WHEN WE FOUND A GOOD DOCTOR AND WE ALL HAD A REAL TALK ABOUT MANAGING MY DIABETES. I HOPED MOM AND DAD WEREN'T GETTING NERVOUS AGAIN.

WE BETTER TELL YOU WHAT'S REALLY GOING ON...

DO YOU REMEMBER WHEN MY COMPANY OPENED THE OFFICE IN STAMFORD?
YES, RIGHT BEFORE WE MOVED HERE.

WELL, THE NEW OFFICE ISN'T GOING WELL. THE COMPANY HAS DECIDED TO CLOSE IT --

OH NO! YOU LOST YOUR JOB!

NOT QUITE. THEY'RE COMBINING THE STAMFORD AND BOSTON OFFICES.
I'M BEING TRANSFERRED BACK TO NEW YORK.

STACEY?

WE KNOW THIS IS A SURPRISE, BUT THINK OF HOW MUCH YOU'VE MISSED NEW YORK.

YEAH... I AM THINKING ABOUT THAT.

THINK OF ALL THE WONDERFUL THINGS WE'LL HAVE WHEN WE MOVE BACK TO THE CITY.
LINCOLN CENTER AND THE METROPOLITAN MUSEUM OF ART...
CENTRAL PARK AND THE NEW YORK PUBLIC LIBRARY!

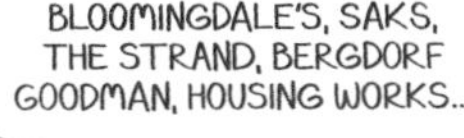
BLOOMINGDALE'S, SAKS, THE STRAND, BERGDORF GOODMAN, HOUSING WORKS...

THAT'S THE SPIRIT!

WHEN ARE WE MOVING?
I HOPE IT'S AT THE END OF THE SCHOOL YEAR. I'M REALLY LOOKING FORWARD TO GRADUATING WITH CLAUDIA.
I'M AFRAID WE CAN'T POSSIBLY WAIT THAT LONG.
THE SCHOOL YEAR DOESN'T END FOR MONTHS. WE'LL BE BACK IN NEW YORK IN FOUR OR FIVE WEEKS.
FOUR OR FIVE WEEKS?!
THE COMPANY WANTS ME BACK AS SOON AS POSSIBLE, AND I PLAN TO DO AS THEY ASK. I FEEL LUCKY THAT WE DON'T HAVE TO PICK UP AND MOVE TO BOSTON.
WE PUT THE HOUSE ON THE MARKET TODAY, AND WE HAVE A REAL ESTATE AGENT LOOKING FOR AN APARTMENT IN NEW YORK.

I ALWAYS DID LIKE HOW BUSY AND FAST THE CITY IS. THERE'S SOMETHING GOING ON AT ALL HOURS OF THE DAY AND NIGHT.

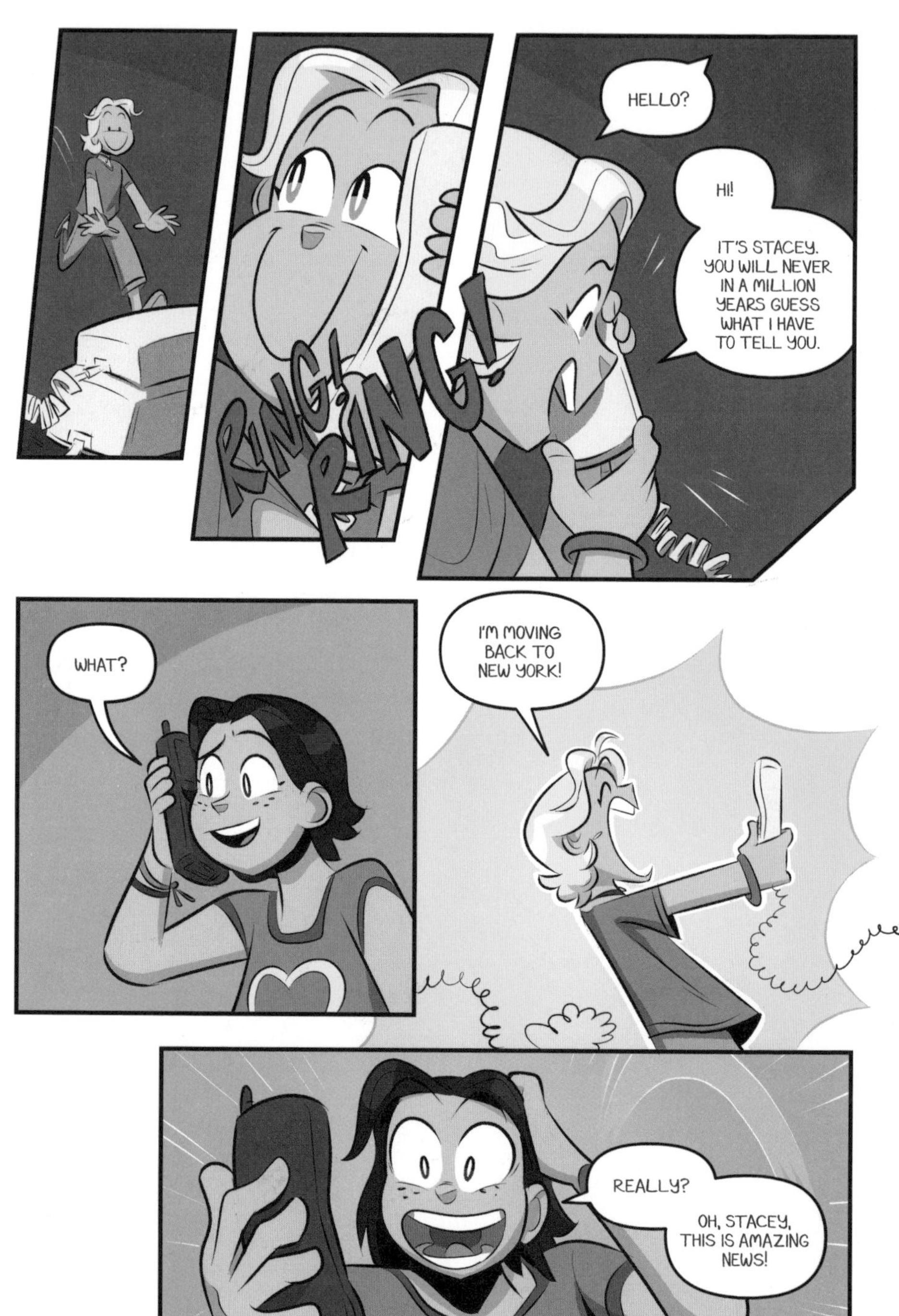
RING! RING!
HELLO?
HI!
IT'S STACEY. YOU WILL NEVER IN A MILLION YEARS GUESS WHAT I HAVE TO TELL YOU.
WHAT?
I'M MOVING BACK TO NEW YORK!
REALLY?
OH, STACEY, THIS IS AMAZING NEWS!

I'LL EVEN BE BACK IN OUR CLASS AT PARKER.

YOU WILL?

YEAH...IS SOMETHING WRONG?

WHO WAS I KIDDING? I COULDN'T WAIT TO GET AWAY FROM NEW YORK AND ALL THOSE FORMER FRIENDS BY THE TIME WE MOVED TO STONEYBROOK.

sniff!

ARE YOU CRYING?

I'M MOVING BACK TO NEW YORK.

WHAT?!
OH, STACE... YOU CAN'T MOVE!

CHAPTER 3

SUCH NEWS!
CLAUDIA WILL MISS YOU. WE ALL WILL.

I CAN'T BELIEVE YOU'RE GOING BACK TO NEW YORK. WELL, OF COURSE I CAN BELIEVE IT, BUT THE NEWS WAS QUITE A SHOCK.

WOULD YOU LIKE TO SIT DOWN FOR A CUP OF TEA?
THANK YOU. I, UM...

MOM, DAD... STACEY AND I WANT TO GO UP TO MY ROOM. WE HAVE A LOT TO TALK ABOUT.
ALL RIGHT. WE UNDERSTAND.

UM, STACE, ARE YOU REALLY MOVING BACK TO NEW YORK? THIS ISN'T SOME BIG JOKE, IS IT?

NOT UNLESS MOM AND DAD ARE PULLING ONE OVER ON ME.
AND THAT'S NOT AT ALL LIKE THEM.

AND YOU'RE MOVING IN A **MONTH?** I JUST CAN'T...I DON'T KNOW.

I DON'T WANT TO LEAVE. I LIKE IT HERE. I'M HAPPY.
THE BABY-SITTERS CLUB WON'T BE IN NEW YORK...YOU WON'T BE IN NEW YORK.
OH, STACEY...

MAYBE IT'LL BE OKAY. WE CAN STILL VISIT EACH OTHER...
BUT IT WON'T BE THE SAME.

CLAUD, DON'T CRY. I'M THE ONE WHO'S MOVING.

I'M THE ONE WHO HAS TO PACK UP HER ROOM, TALK TO HER TEACHERS, AND...QUIT THE BABY-SITTERS CLUB.

WAAAAAH!

OH.

STACE, I DON'T KNOW IF I EVER TOLD YOU THIS, BUT...

YES?
I HAD NEVER CONNECTED SO MUCH WITH ANYONE BEFORE YOU MOVED HERE.
WHAT AM I GOING TO DO WITHOUT YOU?

YOU'RE TRYING TO THINK OF A WAY TO STAY HERE IN STONEYBROOK.

THAT'S RIGHT!

I KNEW IT!

CLAUD, MAYBE I REALLY CAN STAY HERE. MAYBE DAD COULD LOOK FOR A NEW JOB IN STAMFORD.

DO YOU THINK HE'D DO THAT?

NO.
WUMP!
OH.

MAYBE YOUR DAD COULD COMMUTE TO NEW YORK, BUT YOUR FAMILY COULD STAY HERE.

NO... TOO FAR.

HEY, WAIT! I ASKED MY PARENTS IF WE COULD PUT OFF THE MOVE UNTIL AFTER THE SCHOOL YEAR. THEY SAID NO, BUT MAYBE...
WHAT?!

MAYBE MOM AND DAD COULD MOVE AND I COULD STAY HERE, AT LEAST UNTIL WE GRADUATE. OR MAYBE EVEN THROUGH THE SUMMER.
STAY HERE?
OH, GREAT IDEA! MOVE IN WITH US!
YOU CAN LIVE IN THE GUEST ROOM. IT'LL BE AWESOME! WE'LL DO OUR HOMEWORK TOGETHER EVERY NIGHT.
I'D BE RIGHT HERE FOR ALL OUR BSC MEETINGS.
WE COULD TRY ON MAKEUP TOGETHER.
GO SHOPPING TOGETHER.
WE'D **NEVER** GET TIRED OF EACH OTHER.
NO, NEVER!

WHY DON'T I GO DOWNSTAIRS AND ASK MY PARENTS, AND YOU STAY HERE AND CALL YOURS?
OKAY!
BOOP! BOOP! BOOP!

FIVE MINUTES LATER
WHAT'D YOUR PARENTS SAY?
NO.

SAME.
IT FIGURES.

HEY, AT LEAST I CAN COME VISIT, RIGHT?
YEAH. WE CAN GO SHOPPING AT BLOOMINGDALE'S.

CAN WE GO TO A CONCERT, TOO?
SURE!
AND TO THE MET?
OF COURSE.

MAYBE THIS WON'T BE SO BAD, THEN.

MAYBE NOT...
BUT I'LL MISS
MY FRIENDS.
AND WE'LL
MISS YOU.

I HAVE TO
TELL KRISTY AND
THE OTHERS. I'LL
HAVE TO LEAVE
THE CLUB.
YOU GUYS
WON'T HAVE A
TREASURER
ANYMORE.

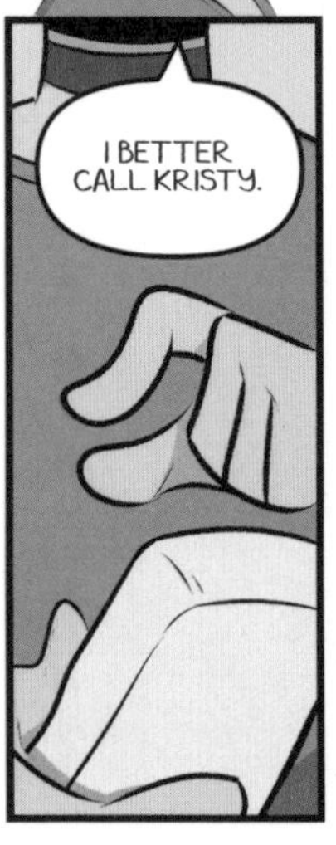
I BETTER
CALL KRISTY.

HELLO,
KRISTY?

IT'S STACEY.
EMERGENCY CLUB
MEETING TOMORROW
IN THE CAFETERIA.

HOME
FOR SALE
CALL:

CHAPTER 4

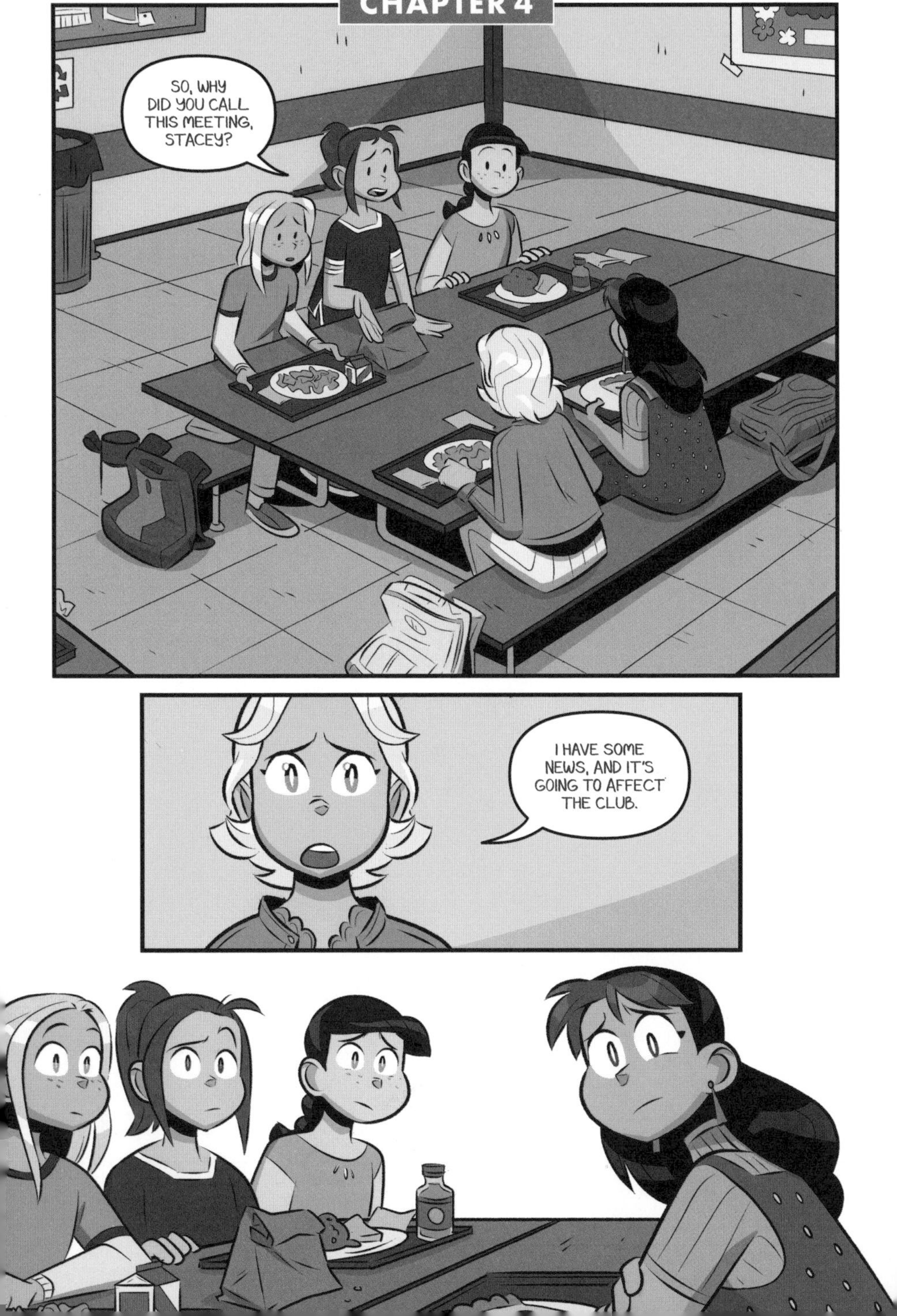

SO, WHY DID YOU CALL THIS MEETING, STACEY?

ARE YOU SICK?
DO YOU HAVE TO GO TO THE HOSPITAL?
OH, NO. I --

DID SOMETHING HAPPEN TO ONE OF YOUR PARENTS? WAIT! NO, DON'T TELL ME. THEY'RE GETTING DIVORCED, RIGHT?
NO, IT'S NOT A DIVORCE.

ARE YOU --
JUST LET HER TALK, OKAY?

WE'RE MOVING.
BACK TO NEW YORK. IN A MONTH.

WE ARE. MY DAD'S COMPANY IS TRANSFERRING HIM, AND IT'S DEFINITE.

THEY'VE ALREADY PUT OUR HOUSE UP FOR SALE, AND THEY'RE LOOKING FOR AN APARTMENT IN THE CITY. EVERYTHING'S GOING TO HAPPEN REALLY FAST.

YOUR ENTHUSIASM IS UNDERWHELMING.
I JUST CAN'T BELIEVE IT. YOU'VE ONLY BEEN HERE FOR...
A LITTLE OVER A YEAR.
WE'VE GOTTEN SO CLOSE...AND HAVE HAD SO MANY ADVENTURES TOGETHER...
I'M REALLY GONNA MISS YOU GUYS...AND THE BSC.
WELL...WHOOPS, I'M LATE! I HAVE TO GO TALK TO MR. ZIZMORE.
HE WANTS TO HELP ME SKIP INTO ALGEBRA BACK AT MY OLD SCHOOL.
BYE!
1

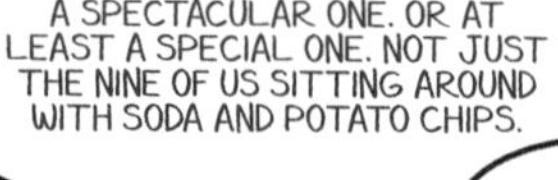
A SPECTACULAR ONE. OR AT LEAST A SPECIAL ONE. NOT JUST THE NINE OF US SITTING AROUND WITH SODA AND POTATO CHIPS.

WE HAVE TO GIVE STACEY A GOING-AWAY PARTY.

WHAT COULD WE DO THAT WOULD BE REALLY SPECIAL?

A SURPRISE PARTY?
A BIG PARTY WITH KIDS FROM SCHOOL?

MAYBE, BUT I'M NOT SURE HOW SPECIAL THOSE IDEAS ARE.

WE MAY HAVE A LITTLE PROBLEM.
WHAT?

WELL, I'M KIND OF LOW ON MONEY, AND I DON'T THINK WE SHOULD USE CLUB FUNDS, SINCE STACEY CONTRIBUTES TO THE TREASURY. IT WOULD BE LIKE SHE WAS PAYING FOR HER OWN PARTY.
OH.

I'VE GOT FIFTEEN.
I'VE GOT TWELVE.

ZERO. I JUST BOUGHT SOME NEW ART SUPPLIES.

THAT WON'T GO VERY FAR IF WE WANT TO GIVE STACEY A REALLY SPECIAL PARTY.
WE'LL HAVE TO THINK OF A WAY TO RAISE MONEY, AND FAST.
FOR STACEY.
FOR STACEY!

Tonight I baby-sat for Jeff Schafer, and we had some discussion. Dawn, you'll especially be interested in it, but I hope it won't upset you when I talk to you about it tomorrow.

The evening got off to a bad start. As soon as you and your mom left, Jeff closed himself in his bedroom. (I guess that isn't so unusual these days.) Anyway, I didn't have much to do, so I sort of wandered around your house. I noticed the living room was a little messy (sorry, but it was), and I started picking things up and putting them away. Everything would have been okay if I hadn't decided to look at one of these pieces of crumpled-up notebook paper that were everywhere. But I did, and Jeff came downstairs just in time to see me. Boy, did he blow up!

Mary Anne

CHAPTER 5

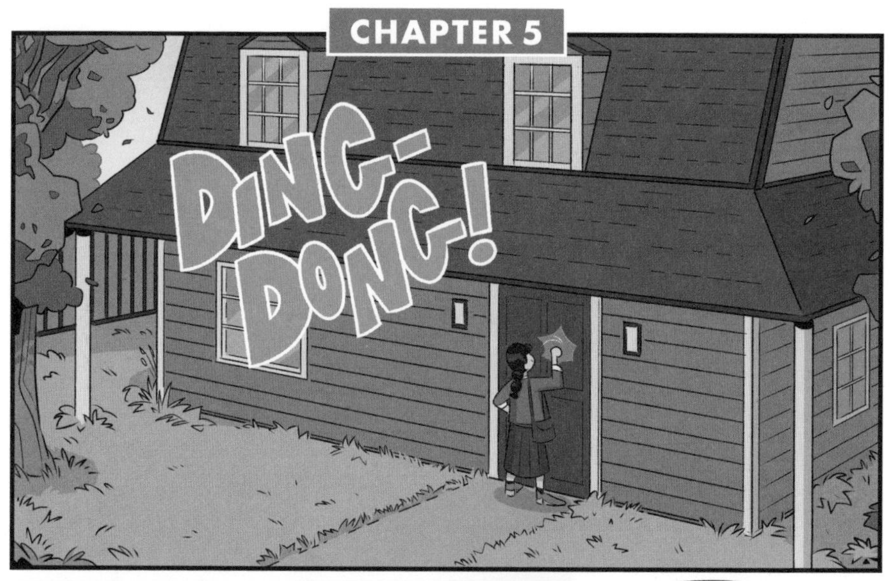

DING-DONG!

YOU'RE EARLY! MOM AND I WERE UPSTAIRS GETTING READY. DON'T ASK ME WHY JEFF COULDN'T COME TO THE DOOR.

IS HE IN ONE OF HIS MOODS AGAIN?
I GUESS SO.

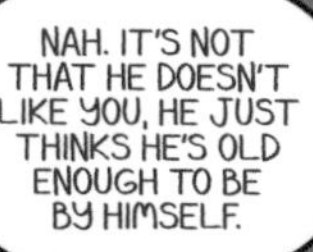

I BET JEFF DIDN'T WANT ME TO BABY-SIT, DID HE?
NAH. IT'S NOT THAT HE DOESN'T LIKE YOU, HE JUST THINKS HE'S OLD ENOUGH TO BE BY HIMSELF.

HMM. WELL, I CAME EARLY TO SEE IF YOU HAVE ANY IDEAS FOR THE PARTY OR FOR GETTING MONEY SO WE CAN HAVE THE PARTY.

I DON'T. HOW ABOUT YOU?
NOT A SINGLE ONE.

WE'LL JUST HAVE TO KEEP THINKING.
DAWN? ARE YOU READY, HONEY?

I'M READY!

BYE!

JEFF?

WELL, I MIGHT AS WELL CLEAN UP A BIT.

WHAT'S THIS?

really want to come stay with you.
California is my home.
w about Mom and Dawn anymore.
I, please? It would be ~~good~~ great.

I WAS TRYING TO WRITE A LETTER. MAIL IS PRIVATE, YOU KNOW. IT'S A FEDERAL OFFENSE TO READ SOMEONE ELSE'S MAIL.

sniff

I'M SORRY THAT I UPSET YOU, JEFF.

I WAS READING YOUR LETTER, BUT I DIDN'T MEAN TO SNOOP. THESE PAPERS WERE JUST LYING ON THE FLOOR.

YOU KNOW, STACEY MCGILL IS MOVING BACK TO NEW YORK CITY.
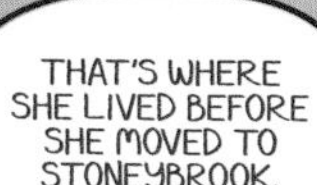

THAT'S WHERE SHE LIVED BEFORE SHE MOVED TO STONEYBROOK.

REALLY?
HOW COME? HER PARENTS AREN'T DIVORCED, ARE THEY?

NOPE. HER FATHER'S COMPANY IS TRANSFERRING HIM. HE HAS TO MOVE BECAUSE OF HIS JOB.

OH.

STACEY REALLY LIKES NEW YORK. SHE'LL MISS HER FRIENDS HERE, BUT, WELL, I THINK DEEP DOWN SHE'S GLAD SHE'S GOING BACK.

I DON'T BLAME HER.

YOUR MOM AND DAWN NEED YOU, TOO. AND YOU NEED THEM.

MY DAD NEEDS ME.

THAT'S DIFFERENT. WE LEFT DAD ALL ALONE OUT IN CALIFORNIA. IF I LIVED WITH DAD, MOM AND DAWN WOULD STILL HAVE EACH OTHER.

BESIDES, MOM AND DAWN TREAT ME LIKE A BABY. DAD DOESN'T DO THAT.

MY DAD USED TO TREAT ME LIKE A **HUGE** BABY.

BUT I THINK HE JUST DID THAT BECAUSE HE LOVES ME.

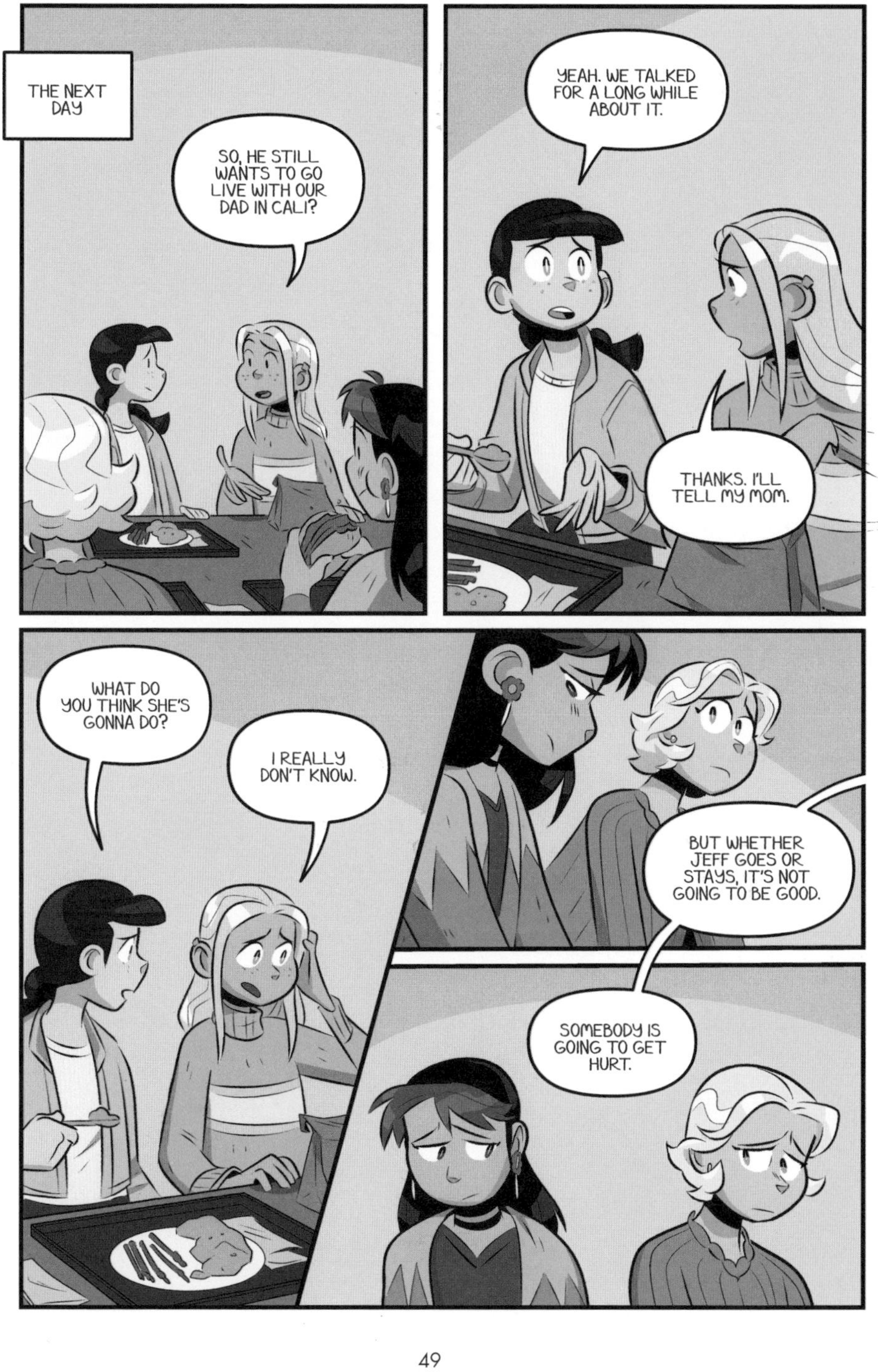

WHAT DO YOU THINK SHE'S GONNA DO?

I REALLY DON'T KNOW.

BUT WHETHER JEFF GOES OR STAYS, IT'S NOT GOING TO BE GOOD.

SOMEBODY IS GOING TO GET HURT.

books
books

CHAPTER 6

I CAN'T --
UGH --

JAM THESE IN...ANY... FARTHER!

HERE, LET ME HELP YOU.

OOF!
THUMP!

STACEY, THAT WORKS WITH SUITCASES FULL OF CLOTHES, NOT BOXES OF BOOKS.

I'LL JUST HAVE TO TAKE SOME OF THESE OUT AND START A NEW BOX.

I UNDERESTIMATED HOW MANY I'D NEED. HOW DID WE ACQUIRE SO MUCH STUFF?

WE THOUGHT THE HOUSE LOOKED EMPTY WHEN WE MOVED HERE, SO WE BOUGHT SOME THINGS TO FILL IT UP. I GUESS WE DID A PRETTY GOOD JOB.
FAR TOO GOOD.

THERE'S NO WAY WE'RE GOING TO FIT EVERYTHING INTO OUR NEW APARTMENT.

YOU KNOW, THERE'S PROBABLY A LOT OF STUFF WE DON'T REALLY NEED...WHY DON'T WE HAVE A YARD SALE?

I DON'T THINK SO, HONEY. HOW CAN I ARRANGE FOR ONE WHEN I HAVE TO PACK AND MAKE CALLS AND --
WHAT IF I RAN THE SALE?
I BET MY FRIENDS WOULD HELP. IT'LL BE FUN.
WELL...IT'S A BIG JOB, YOU KNOW.
YOU HAVE TO PRICE EVERYTHING, TAG ALL THE ITEMS, SET THEM UP IN THE YARD, AND ADVERTISE.
PLEASE, MOM? YOU KNOW WE CAN HANDLE IT.

YOU'RE RIGHT, HONEY.
IF YOU AND YOUR FRIENDS WILL ORGANIZE AND RUN THE ENTIRE SALE, YOU CAN KEEP WHATEVER MONEY YOU MAKE.

ARE YOU KIDDING?! OH, THANKS!

IT MIGHT BE A LOT OF MONEY, THOUGH, MOM.

RING!
RING!
HELLO?
OH...MIMI? SORRY, IT'S STACEY. I THOUGHT I HAD CALLED CLAUDIA'S LINE.
IS CLAUDIA HOME?
...MARY ANNE'S? ALL RIGHT, THANKS. BYE.
CLICK!

HI, GUYS! SORRY, MIMI TOLD ME YOU WERE HERE, AND I WANTED TO TELL YOU THE NEWS.

WHAT IS IT?

MY MOM'S LETTING US ORGANIZE A YARD SALE TO GET RID OF OUR JUNK -- AND WE GET TO KEEP THE MONEY!

WOW, THAT'S TERRIFIC!

DO WE REALLY GET TO KEEP THE MONEY?

OOF!

ALL OF IT. WE'LL SPLIT IT SEVEN WAYS.

I FEEL KIND OF FUNNY TAKING MONEY FOR SELLING **YOUR** THINGS...

LISTEN, IT'S A FAVOR TO MY PARENTS.
PLEASE?

THAT SOUNDS LIKE FUN!
OF COURSE WE'LL HELP.
ANYTHING FOR YOU, STACE.
YEAH! I LOVE SELLING STUFF.
WE CAN MAKE POSTERS TO PUT UP IN THE NEIGHBORHOOD.
YEAH, EVERYONE WILL COME OVER!

I BETTER GO HOME. MOM AND I NEED TO START GETTING THE SALE ITEMS TOGETHER.

I'LL SEE YOU GUYS LATER!

AT THE TIME, I WAS TOO EXCITED ABOUT THE YARD SALE TO WONDER WHY THEY WERE MEETING WITHOUT ME.

RING
RING
HELLO?
STACEY, HI! IT'S ME, LAINE. GUESS WHAT.
AS A WELCOME BACK PRESENT, MY DAD GOT TICKETS FOR YOU AND ME TO SEE *MAD ABOUT MILLIE!*
NO! REALLY? OH, THAT'S FANTASTIC! THANK YOU!
I'VE GOT SOME EXCITING NEWS, TOO. MY MATH TEACHER IS GETTING ME READY FOR ALGEBRA!
MAYBE WE'LL BE IN THE SAME CLASS!

OH. SUPER. UM, WE WILL, SINCE THERE'S ONLY ONE EIGHTH-GRADE ALGEBRA CLASS...
AND ALLISON RITZ IS IN IT, TOO.

SHE IS?!

HAS SHE SAID ANYTHING ABOUT MY COMING BACK?

WELL...SHE SORT OF SAID, "OH, GREAT, BARF-MOUTH IS RETURNING."
YEAH, FROM THAT TIME YOU GOT SICK IN THE CAFETERIA? BEFORE YOU WERE ON INSULIN.
BARF-MOUTH?!

MAYBE I SHOULD ASK MR. ZIZMORE TO KEEP ME OUT OF ALGEBRA.
STACE, NO. I WANT YOU IN OUR CLASS.

THANKS, LAINE.
UM, I'VE GOT SOME PACKING TO DO. CAN I CALL YOU LATER?

SURE THING. BYE.
JUST A MINUTE AGO, I HAD BEEN HAPPY AND EXCITED. NOW I WAS SAD AND WORRIED.

Click!
DID I WANT TO GO BACK TO NEW YORK OR NOT?
I WISHED I COULD DIVIDE MYSELF AND LIVE HALF IN STONEYBROOK, HALF IN MANHATTAN.

555-5309
1)
2)
3)
NEED A TOASTER?
NEED A COASTER?
NEVER FUSS,
COME SEE US!
NEED A PAIL?
NEED A SNAIL?
THEN BE HASTY,
COME SEE STACEY!
a responsible
S
C
-6:00 pm
555-0457
555-0457
Ba

CHAPTER 7

WHAT DO YOU THINK?

WELL, THE ART IS WONDERFUL, CLAUD. I LOVE THE SNAIL WITH HIS ANTENNAE, AND THE HOUSE ON HIS BACK INSTEAD OF A SHELL...

BUT...?

BUT THE POETRY STINKS.

HASTY AND STACEY DON'T RHYME. ALSO, WE DON'T HAVE ANY SNAILS FOR SALE.
WELL, MAYBE WE SHOULD.

GUYS, WE DON'T REALLY HAVE TIME FOR ARGUMENTS.

AND, CLAUDIA, YOU ILLUSTRATE THE ADS. NOBODY CAN DRAW AS WELL AS YOU.

ALL RIGHT.

OKAY! LET'S GET TO WORK!

GA

Sketch

PHEW. I'M THIRSTY. DOES ANYONE ELSE WANT A DRINK?

ONLY IF YOU'VE GOT SOME SODA THAT'S JUST BRIMMING WITH ARTIFICIAL COLORING.

AND BIGLUDIUM EXFORBINATE.
hehe

WE'VE PROBABLY GOT SOMETHING LIKE THAT. I'M GOING TO HAVE ICED TEA, THOUGH.

OH, I'LL SECOND THAT.
I'LL HAVE ICED TEA, TOO.
ME TOO!

HA, THANKS.
I'LL HELP YOU WITH THE GLUTIOUS EXORBITANTS.

YOU KNOW, I HAVEN'T TOLD CHARLOTTE THAT I'M MOVING.

YOU HAVEN'T?
I GUESS I'VE BEEN PUTTING IT OFF.

YOU BETTER TELL HER SOON. I MEAN, THE ADS FOR THE YARD SALE WILL BE A MAJOR CLUE.
DON'T YOU THINK SHE SHOULD FIND OUT FROM YOU AND NOT FROM A SNAIL?

I GUESS SO. IT'S NOT GOING TO BE EASY, THOUGH.

NO, I SUPPOSE IT WON'T BE. IF SHE FEELS ANYTHING LIKE ME...

WELL, WE BETTER GO BACK UPSTAIRS.
YEAH. KRISTY'S WAITING TO BE BIGLUDIUM EXFORBINATED.

THANKS FOR THE DRINKS.
NO PROBLEM!
HOW'S IT COMING ALONG WITH THE ADS?
WE'RE FINISHED! LISTEN:
WE'RE MOVING BACK TO NEW YORK CITY, WE KNOW IT'S GOING TO BE HARD...
BUT THINGS WILL BE A LITTLE BIT BETTER IF YOU'LL COME TO THE SALE IN OUR YARD.
NOW THAT'S AN AD.
GREAT JOB, YOU GUYS!
ALL RIGHT, DOWN TO THE BASEMENT. WAIT'LL YOU SEE WHAT MOM BOUGHT FOR US THIS MORNING.

WHAT IS IT?
YOU'LL SEE.

WHOA. THAT'S A LOT OF JUNK.
YUP. AND WE'RE GONNA PRICE IT...
WITH THESE.
WHAT ARE THEY?
PRICE TAGS! BLANK ONES. WE'LL HAVE TO WRITE IN THE PRICE WE DECIDE FOR EACH ITEM.
AWESOME! THIS SALE IS GOING TO LOOK SO PROFESSIONAL.

OKAY, LET'S START.
WHAT DO YOU GUYS THINK? FORTY DOLLARS?

FORTY!
ARE YOU KIDDING?

WELL, MOM MUST'VE PAID A LOT FOR IT, AND IT'S ONLY A YEAR OLD. FORTY DOLLARS IS A STEAL.

NOT AT A YARD SALE, IT ISN'T.

ARE YOU SURE?

DAWN, HAVE YOU EVER BEEN TO A YARD SALE?

NO...

WELL, TRUST ME. IF YOU PRICE THIS AT FORTY DOLLARS, OUR CUSTOMERS WILL LAUGH US RIGHT OUT OF THE YARD.
TWO BUCKS.
WHAT?! THIRTY DOLLARS.
TWENTY?
THREE.
THREE FIFTY.
KRISTY!
FINE...

HOW ARE WE SUPPOSED TO EARN ANY MONEY?
WE WILL. YOU'LL SEE.

LET'S GET TO WORK!

HEYYY...
I HAVE AN IDEA.
WHAT IS IT?
LET'S MAKE THIS YARD SALE MORE THAN JUST A REGULAR YARD SALE. LET'S SELL LEMONADE, TOO.
AND HOW ABOUT THOSE GREAT BROWNIES I BAKE?
AND HANDMADE STUFF!
LIKE POTHOLDERS AND SCARVES.
WHAT ABOUT BABIES FROM MY SPIDER PLANTS?
YEAH!
THIS YARD SALE IS GOING TO GO DOWN IN HISTORY AS THE BEST EVER!

Jewelry:
$1 / piece
75¢
75¢
75¢
$3
50¢
50¢

CHAPTER 8

THE NEXT DAY
I NEEDED TO TELL CHARLOTTE THAT I WAS MOVING. I FELT AWFUL.
DING-
HI, STACEY!

I GOT THREE GOLD STARS IN SCHOOL TODAY! I HAVE TWENTY-ONE ALTOGETHER.
WHEN YOU HAVE TWENTY-FIVE, YOU GET TO BE THE TEACHER'S HELPER FOR ONE WHOLE DAY!
THAT'S WONDERFUL, CHARLOTTE! I'M REALLY PROUD OF YOU!
THANKS. REMEMBER LAST YEAR WHEN I HATED SCHOOL? NOW IT'S THE FUNNEST THING EVER.
AND GUESS WHO MY BEST FRIEND IS.
HMM, I GIVE UP.
VALERIE NAMM. SHE'S THE MOST POPULAR GIRL IN THE WHOLE FOURTH GRADE AND --

CHARLOTTE, EXCUSE ME, HONEY.

LET STACEY COME INSIDE. I NEED TO SPEAK TO HER FOR A MINUTE, OKAY? THEN YOU TWO CAN TALK ALL AFTERNOON.
OKAY.

WHY DON'T YOU GO UPSTAIRS AND FIND THE PLANET CHART YOU MADE? I THINK STACEY WOULD LIKE TO SEE IT.
YEAH!

...

DR. JOHANSSEN --
STACEY --

ha ha
YOU GO.

WELL...
I HEARD THAT YOUR FAMILY IS MOVING. AND THEN I DROVE BY YOUR HOUSE AND SAW THE FOR SALE SIGN.

THAT WAS WHAT I WANTED TO TALK TO YOU ABOUT. WE **ARE** MOVING. I WAS GOING TO TELL CHARLOTTE EVERYTHING TODAY. IF THAT'S OKAY WITH YOU.

OH, IT'S FINE, STACEY. THANK YOU. YOU'RE SO RESPONSIBLE, AND BOY, ARE WE GOING TO MISS YOU.

BELIEVE ME, I'M GOING TO MISS YOU, TOO.
GOOD LUCK.

BYE, CHAR. I'M GOING TO THE HOSPITAL NOW. DADDY WILL BE HOME AT SIX.
OKAY! BYE, MOM!
I COULDN'T FIND THE PLANET CHART.
GOOD THING I BROUGHT MY KID-KIT.
WHAT'S IN IT TODAY?
SOME OF THE SAME STUFF AND A FEW NEW THINGS, INCLUDING A NEW BOOK.
OH, GOODY. WE NEED ONE NOW THAT WE'RE DONE WITH *THE BORROWERS*.
MORGAN'S MESSY MOVE
THAT'S A FUNNY TITLE.
WHAT'S IT ABOUT?

WELL, IT'S ABOUT A FAMILY THAT MOVES AWAY.
THE LAST TIME I MOVED I WAS TWO. I DON'T REMEMBER IT AT ALL.

THE LAST TIME I MOVED WAS WHEN I MOVED HERE. THAT WAS JUST ONE YEAR AGO. A YEAR AND A COUPLE OF MONTHS.
I'M GLAD YOU MOVED HERE.
ME TOO. BUT...

I HAVE TO TELL YOU SOMETHING, CHARLOTTE. WE'RE MOVING AGAIN.
WHAT?

WE'RE MOVING BACK TO NEW YORK IN A COUPLE OF WEEKS.

YOU MEAN YOU'RE LEAVING STONEYBROOK? YOU'RE LEAVING ME?

I'M REALLY SORRY, CHAR.
I DON'T WANT TO GO. BUT MY DAD'S JOB IS CHANGING. WE HAVE TO MOVE.
I HATE YOU!
I HATE YOU! YOU'RE MEAN! I THOUGHT YOU LIKED BABY-SITTING FOR ME.
I DO. I LOVE IT.
THAT DOESN'T HAVE ANYTHING TO DO WITH THE MOVE. IT'S MY DAD'S JOB, JUST LIKE I TOLD YOU. I WISH I COULD STAY IN STONEYBROOK, TOO.

HEY. WOULD YOU LIKE TO COME OVER TO MY HOUSE?
OKAY. BUT WHY?
I'LL SHOW YOU WHAT'S GOING ON OVER THERE. YOU MIGHT THINK IT'S INTERESTING. WE HAVE TO PACK UP EVERY SINGLE THING IN THE HOUSE.
Dr. Johanssen,
I've taken Charlotte for a quick visit to my house. Will be back soon!
Stacey
MAYBE THAT WOULD HELP HER UNDERSTAND THINGS.
WHERE WILL YOU FIND ENOUGH BOXES?
THE MOVING COMPANY GIVES THEM TO US. YOU'LL SEE. SOME OF THEM ARE FULL ALREADY.

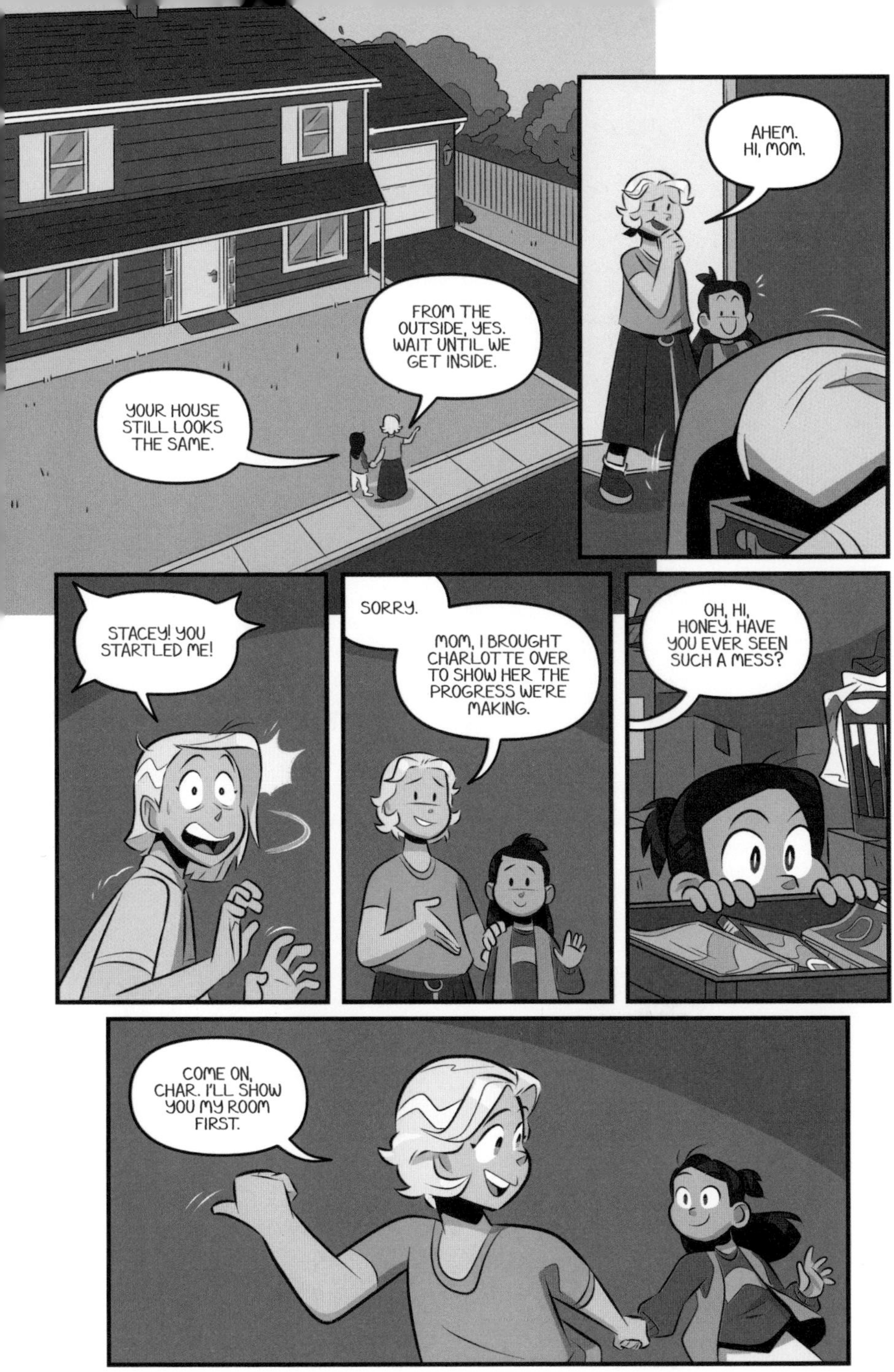

YOUR HOUSE STILL LOOKS THE SAME.

FROM THE OUTSIDE, YES. WAIT UNTIL WE GET INSIDE.

AHEM. HI, MOM.

HUH. THIS DOESN'T LOOK TOO DIFFERENT.
I KNOW. MOM KEEPS TELLING ME TO "GET CRACKING." LET'S GO LOOK AT MY PARENTS' ROOM.
WHOA.
I HOPE YOU'RE MOVING TO ANOTHER BIG HOUSE.
WE'RE NOT.
WE'RE MOVING INTO AN APARTMENT, SO WE'RE GETTING RID OF OUR EXTRA STUFF WITH A BIG YARD SALE.
A YARD SALE!
I **LOVE** YARD SALES. I GOT A BARBIE DOLL AND A DOLLHOUSE AT A YARD SALE IN SHERIDAN, AND YOU KNOW HOW MUCH BOTH OF THEM COST? JUST TWO DOLLARS!
winter
coats
shoes

COME ON DOWN TO THE BASEMENT. YOU CAN SEE HOW WE'RE GETTING READY FOR OUR YARD SALE.
IF THERE'S SOMETHING YOU WANT, I'LL SET IT ASIDE FOR YOU.
YAY! LET'S GO!
WHOA. THIS SURE IS A LOT OF STUFF.
YEAH, THAT'S WHY THE BABY-SITTERS CLUB MEMBERS ARE GOING TO HELP ME RUN THE SALE.
SEE? WE'RE TAGGING EVERYTHING AND WRITING DOWN THE PRICES.
AND WE'RE MAKING ADS. IN A COUPLE OF DAYS WE'RE GOING TO PASS THEM OUT TO THE NEIGHBORS.
COOL!

SEE ANYTHING YOU LIKE?
HMM...

THE CRICKET IN TIMES SQUARE
By George Selden

REMEMBER WHEN WE READ THIS TOGETHER?
SURE I DO. THAT WAS FUN.
THE CRICKET IN TIMES SQUARE
By George Selden

SAVE IT FOR ME, OKAY? THAT'S WHAT I WANT YOU TO PUT ASIDE.
THE CRICKET IN TIMES SQUARE
By George Selden

I'LL DO BETTER THAN THAT.

Love to Charlotte,
My Favorite Kid,
From Stacey,
Her Favorite Baby-sitter

THIS AFTERNOON, BUDDY AND SUZI BARRETT LEARNED A BUSINESS LESSON. UNFORTUNATELY, IT WAS SORT OF A HARD LESSON, BUT IN THE END EVERYTHING WORKED OUT OKAY. BETTER THAN OKAY, EVEN. (I WISH I COULD BE MORE SPECIFIC RIGHT NOW, BUT I CAN'T.)

ANYWAY, BUDDY AND SUZI HAD COME UP WITH WHAT THEY THOUGHT WAS A GREAT WAY TO EARN SOME MONEY. THEY'D GOTTEN THE IDEA WHEN THEY SAW THE ADS FOR STACEY'S YARD SALE. THE THING WAS, BUSY MRS. BARRETT DIDN'T WANT TO BE AROUND WHEN BUDDY AND SUZI PUT THEIR PLAN INTO ACTION. SHE LEFT THE PROJECT FOR WHEN I WAS BABY-SITTING. (SHE DID PAY ME EXTRA FOR MY TROUBLE, THOUGH.)

-DAWN

CHAPTER 9

DING-DONG!

HI, DAWN!
HI, BUDDY. HI, SUZI. HI, MARNIE.

HI, DAWN. I TOLD BUDDY AND SUZI THEY COULD HOLD A SIDEWALK SALE TODAY.
I'M HEADING OUT. YOU KNOW WHERE THE PHONE NUMBERS ARE.
WE SAW THE POSTERS FOR STACEY'S YARD SALE. WE WANNA HAVE ONE, TOO!
BACK AT SIX! BYE, KIDS!
HUH?
WAIT A SEC!

MRS. BARRETT! WHAT ARE THEY SELLING?
EVERYTHING IS ON THE LIVING ROOM FLOOR!
ARE THE ITEMS PRICED?
NO. YOU CAN HELP THEM WITH THAT.
WHAT ARE WE GOING TO SET UP THE STUFF ON?
OH. THERE'S A BLANKET IN THE FRONT HALL CLOSET.
WHAT ABOUT MARNIE?
PUT HER IN THE PLAYPEN. IT'S IN THE REC ROOM.

skkrrrreeee
HAVE FUN!

OH, BROTHER.

IT'S SIDEWALK SALE DAY!
LET'S GET STARTED, DAWN!
WAIT A SEC, GUYS. LET ME TAKE CARE OF MARNIE FIRST.
gurrrgle

POOR MARNIE-O. YOU DEFINITELY NEED A CHANGE.
NO-NO.

ALL RIGHT. ARE YOU READY TO BE A SALES BABY?
NO-NO.
THAT'S THE SPIRIT.

OKAY, GUYS. LET'S SET UP!

LOOKS GREAT!
I GUESS YOU'RE IN BUSINESS!

WHAT SHOULD WE DO FIRST?
I THINK YOU SHOULD SORT OF ARRANGE THE STUFF ON THE BLANKET.
YOU KNOW, FIX IT UP SO IT LOOKS LIKE A REAL STORE, ALL NICE AND NEAT, AND LIKE YOU'D WANT TO BUY SOMETHING.
AND SET IT UP SO PEOPLE CAN FIND WHAT THEY'RE LOOKING FOR.
OKAY, ALL FINISHED!
WHERE ARE OUR CUSTOMERS?

YOU NEED A SIGN, I THINK.
Toy SaLe
Come one, come ALL
THERE WE GO.

HEY!

TOY SALE! BUY OUR TOYS!

HEY, SLOW DOWN!
STOP! STOP!!

HOW COME NO ONE IS STOPPING?

HM. I THINK THE PROBLEM IS THAT NO ONE KNEW ABOUT THE SALE AHEAD OF TIME.

WE TOLD THE PIKES ABOUT IT.

HI, DAWN!

MARGO

CLAIRE

VANESSA

OH! WELL, HERE THEY COME.

HI, GUYS.

I THINK I'D LIKE TO BUY THE TOW TRUCK. I COULD GIVE IT TO NICKY FOR HIS BIRTHDAY.
HOW MUCH IS IT?
TWO DOLLARS.
FIVE CENTS.
HOW MUCH?
I THINK YOU SHOULD CHARGE THEM TWENTY-FIVE CENTS.
TWENTY-FIVE CENTS?!
WELL, IT'S USED AND VERY TINY.
OKAY...
SEE YOU LATER!
THANK YOU!

THAT WAS OUR ONLY SALE.

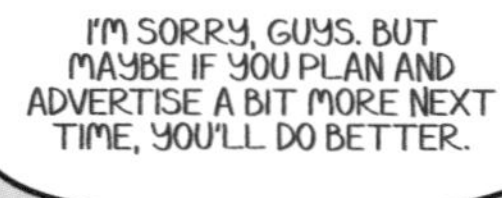
I'M SORRY, GUYS. BUT MAYBE IF YOU PLAN AND ADVERTISE A BIT MORE NEXT TIME, YOU'LL DO BETTER.

YEAH...

HEY, HOW ABOUT YOU COME SELL YOUR TOYS AT STACEY'S YARD SALE THIS SATURDAY?
YOU CAN SET UP A BOOTH BY THE GARAGE.

THAT WOULD BE GREAT!

HOW COME STACEY'S HAVING A YARD SALE?
SHE'S MOVING BACK TO NEW YORK SOON.

WILL YOU MISS HER?
I SURE WILL. ALL HER FRIENDS WILL. WE'RE GOING TO GIVE HER A BIG PARTY BEFORE SHE LEAVES.
A PARTY! CAN WE COME?
Crash!
HONK HONK!
I HOPE SO! I'LL TALK TO YOUR MOM ABOUT IT.
BYE, DAWN!

SUZI HAD GIVEN DAWN AN IDEA.
BEEP BEEP!
HELLO?
KRISTY, IT'S DAWN.

I THOUGHT OF A SPECIAL, MEANINGFUL, AND **WONDERFUL** PARTY FOR STACEY.

OH, THANK GOODNESS. I WAS REALLY GETTING WORRIED.

TELL ME!

YARD
Sale!

CHAPTER 10

I DIDN'T KNOW IF IT'S POSSIBLE TO FEEL NERVOUS WHEN YOU'RE ASLEEP...
BUT THAT MUST'VE BEEN WHAT WAS HAPPENING, BECAUSE WHEN I OPENED MY EYES, THE BUTTERFLIES WERE ALREADY THERE.
tick tick
RIIIN-!!

A SUNNY DAY.
PERFECT FOR
A YARD SALE.

I STILL HAD SO MUCH TO DO BEFORE THEN!
WHOA, SLOW DOWN!

OH NO! WE DON'T HAVE ANY CHANGE!

WHAT IF THE VERY FIRST CUSTOMER PAYS FOR A FIFTY CENT TOY WITH A FIVE DOLLAR BILL?

RELAX. I'LL GIVE YOU TEN DOLLARS IN CHANGE.

YOU CAN PAY ME BACK WHEN THE SALE'S OVER.

OH, THANK YOU!

DING-DONG

THEY'RE HERE!
AND THEY CAME BEARING GOODIES!
BROWNIES
KNITTED ITEMS
LEMONADE AND LIMEADE MIX
SPIDER PLANTS

WE'VE GOT THIS.

LET'S GET TO WORK!

THE NIGHT BEFORE, MY FRIENDS HAD BROUGHT OVER A TON OF STUFF FROM THEIR OWN HOUSES.

WHOA. WE BETTER GET STARTED.

Yard Sale!

ITCHEN
refreshments

NOW FOR THE SALE STUFF.
LET'S HAUL IT OUT OF THE BASEMENT FIRST AND THEN WORRY ABOUT THE PLANTS AND THE FOOD.
LET ME GET MY DAD TO HELP WITH THE BIG STUFF!

NOW WE CAN ARRANGE EVERYTHING NICELY.
JUST LIKE AT THE MALL!
Hats
15
TWEENS
Man-Dog
AMETHYST
Books
NINE THIRTY-FIVE!
PEOPLE WILL BE HERE IN TWENTY-FIVE MINUTES!

THE LEMONADE'S NOT MIXED. OR THE LIMEADE. CLAUDIA, YOU HAVE TO CUT THE BROWNIES INTO SQUARES! WHERE ARE THE NAPKINS? AND WHO'S GOING TO BE IN CHARGE OF SETTING UP FOR THE BARRETTS?

STACE, RELAX.

YOU AND CLAUDIA FOCUS ON THE FOOD AND DRINKS WHILE THE REST OF US FINISH SETTING UP.

9:40

9:55
refreshments
prices:
LEMONADE!
WE MADE IT!

EVERYONE RAN TO THEIR STATIONS.
IT LOOKED LIKE WE OPENED RIGHT IN THE NICK OF TIME.
HI, MRS. PREZZIOSO!
HI, EVERYONE!
OUT

I HOPE YOU DON'T MIND THAT WE'RE A FEW MINUTES EARLY.
WE ALWAYS LIKE TO GET TO SALES FIRST SO WE CAN HAVE THE PICK OF THE LITTER, IF YOU KNOW WHAT I MEAN.
OF COURSE.
OH, LOVELY.
A REAL FIND.
THAT'LL BE FIVE DOLLARS.
OUR FIRST SALE!
I JUST LOVE SELLING THINGS AND MAKING MONEY.
THIS IS GOING TO BE A GREAT DAY!

HI, MR. SPIER!
GOOD MORNING!
BEFORE I KNEW IT, OUR DRIVEWAY HAD FILLED UP!

THEN THE QUESTIONS BEGAN FLYING.
WOULD YOU SAY THE PING-PONG TABLE IS IN GOOD CONDITION?
DEFINITELY. IT'S ONLY SIX MONTHS OLD, AND WE DIDN'T USE IT MUCH.

IS THIS STATUE MADE OF MARBLE?
NO, JUST FANCY CEMENT.

HOW OLD IS THE PRINTER?
UM, LET ME ASK MY DAD.
tech

THANKFULLY, MY FRIENDS WERE A BIG HELP.
ARE THE SHUTTERS FOR SALE?
NO, I'M SORRY. THEY'RE NOT.

HOW MUCH IS THIS RING?
I WANT TO SURPRISE DORIANNE WITH IT.
I'LL HANDLE THIS.

THESE BROWNIES ARE SIMPLY DELICIOUS!
THANK YOU!

WE EVEN HAD SOME SURPRISE VISITORS!
HI, EVERYONE.
SHANNON AND LOGAN!
HOWDY.
HI.
WHERE CAN SOMEONE GET A GREAT SCARF AROUND HERE?
YOU'RE IN LUCK. I HAVE ONE SAVED JUST FOR YOU.
LOGAN IS MARY ANNE'S BOYFRIEND.
I'VE GOT SOMETHING FOR YOU, TOO.
WELL, FOR ASTRID.
SHE'LL LOVE IT. WE SHOULD HAVE A PUPPY PLAYDATE SOMETIME.
YEAH!

PEOPLE CAME AND WENT, AND THE DAY FLEW BY.
11

Hats
Yard Sale

SOON ENOUGH, IT WAS TIME TO CLOSE UP SHOP.
HEY, STACE? WE'RE OUT OF INVENTORY.
I THINK WE SHOULD BREAK IT DOWN, UNLESS YOU'RE WAITING ON SOMEONE.

I **WAS** HOPING TO SEE ONE MORE PERSON...

YEAH, WE PROBABLY SHOULD.

STACEY?

CHARLOTTE! I'M GLAD YOU CAME!

STACEY, YOU KNOW I LOVE YARD SALES.

BUT I JUST DIDN'T WANT TO COME AFTER ALL. I DIDN'T WANT TO SEE YOU SELLING YOUR THINGS. THAT'S WHY I'M LATE.

AND...I DON'T WANT TO BUY ANYTHING. I WANT TO GIVE YOU THIS.

The Girl Who Moved Away
By: Charlotte Johanssen
Dedication:
This book is for my favorite baby-sitter from her favorite kid.
To remember me by.
—C.J.

AFTER WE CLEANED UP, THE BSC STAYED TO HELP ADD UP OUR PROFITS.
PIZZA

CARRY THE ONE...OKAY, GOT IT.

EVEN AFTER PAYING MY DAD BACK THE TEN DOLLARS, WE MADE JUST OVER...

FIVE HUNDRED DOLLARS!
AHHHHHHHH!!!

WHOA!
AWESOME!

I NEVER WOULD'VE BEEN ABLE TO DO THIS WITHOUT YOUR HELP. THANK YOU.

CHAPTER 11

Dear Stacey,

You are cordially invited to a farewell party in your honor this Saturday at two o'clock P.M.

It will be at Kristy's house. Important! Wear old clothes!

Please RSVP.

Sincerely,
The Baby-sitters Club

WE USUALLY DON'T MAIL OUT PARTY INVITATIONS. WE JUST CALL.

AND WHY DID THE NOTE SAY TO WEAR OLD CLOTHES? WHAT WERE WE GOING TO DO? PAINT KRISTY'S ROOM?

SOMETHING WAS DEFINITELY UP.

SATURDAY

NICE OUTFIT.

GLAD I'M NOT UNDERDRESSED.

THE PARTY'S OUT BACK.

NOW, CLOSE YOUR EYES.

SURPRISE!!!

OH, WOW!

DID WE SURPRISE YOU?
YOU SURE DID.

THESE FLOWERS ARE FOR YOU.

TODAY IS YOUR SPECIAL DAY. WE ARE ALL HERE TO HONOR YOU, TO SAY GOOD-BYE, AND TO...

HAVE FUN!!!

THIS IS A PARTY NOT JUST FOR STACEY, BUT FOR EVERYBODY HERE. SO...
LET THE FUN BEGIN!
WHAT ARE WE GOING TO DO FIRST?
WE'RE GOING TO HAVE AN EGG RELAY RACE.
EVERYONE TO THEIR STATIONS!

I COULDN'T BELIEVE HOW PREPARED MY FRIENDS WERE. THE KIDS' TEAMS WERE ORGANIZED AND READY IN THE BLINK OF AN EYE!
FWEEEE!!
SPLAT!
I CAN SEE WHY WE WERE SUPPOSED TO WEAR OLD CLOTHES.

Clunk!
Double SQUISH!
I WON! I WON!
YOU MEAN, WE WON.

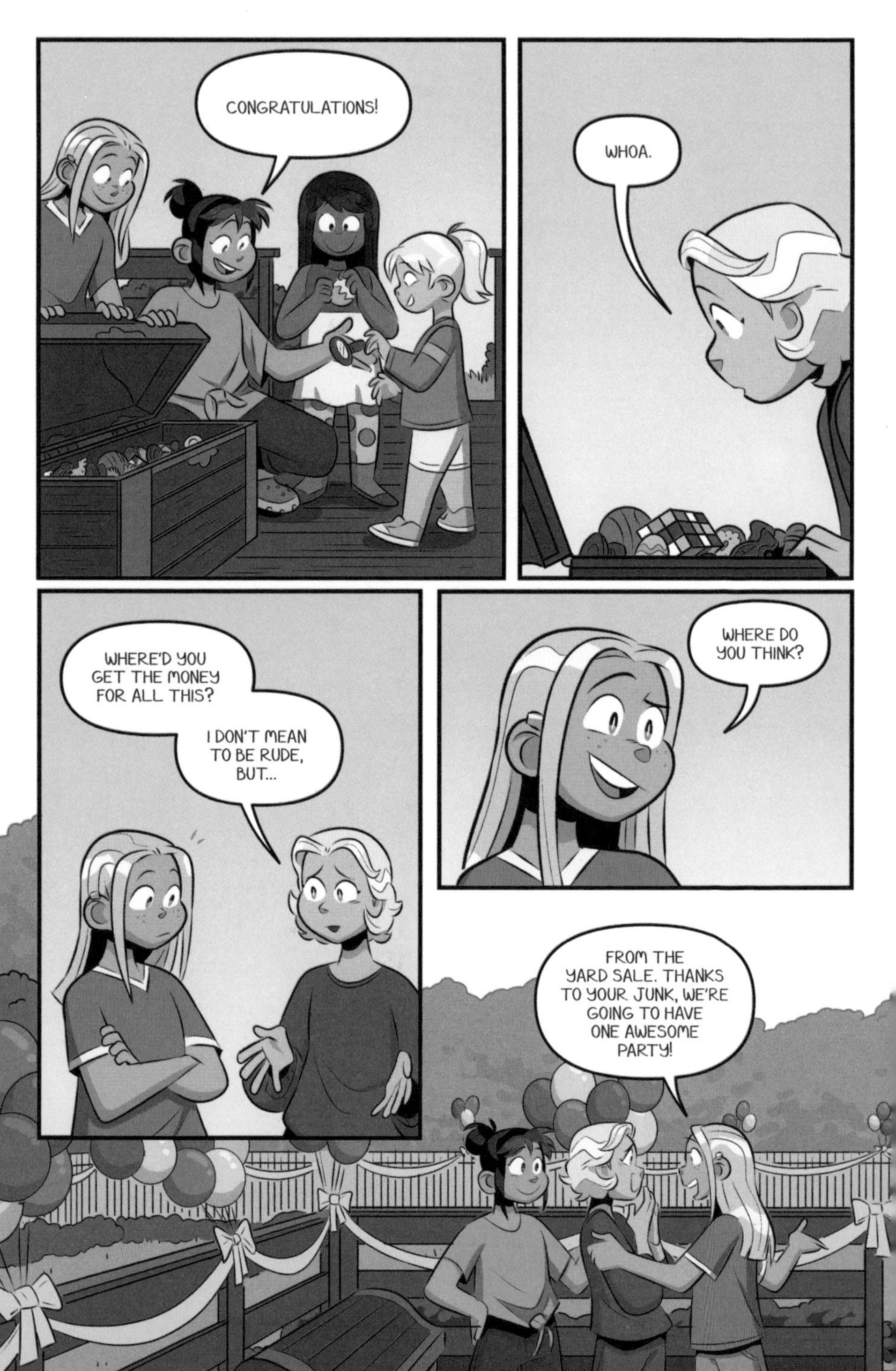
CONGRATULATIONS!
WHOA.
WHERE'D YOU GET THE MONEY FOR ALL THIS?
I DON'T MEAN TO BE RUDE, BUT...
WHERE DO YOU THINK?
FROM THE YARD SALE. THANKS TO YOUR JUNK, WE'RE GOING TO HAVE ONE AWESOME PARTY!

OH MY GOSH, REALLY? THAT'S SO THOUGHTFUL!

ANYTHING FOR YOU.
YOU'RE TOO MUCH.

ALL RIGHT! TIME FOR OUR NEXT EVENT!

THE NEXT HOUR
WENT BY IN A BLUR.

TIME TO QUIET DOWN. WE'VE GOT ONE LAST ACTIVITY.
CAN YOU GUYS HELP ME?

SO, WE'RE GOING TO DRAW HER A BIG PICTURE OF OUR TOWN. YOU CAN PUT IN YOUR STREETS AND YOUR HOUSES AND YOURSELVES. THEN STACEY WILL ALWAYS REMEMBER US.

THIS CAME OUT GREAT. GOOD JOB!

farewell to you, farewell to you
farewell dear Stacey
farewell and good luck

OH! YOU GUYS...
Good-Bye, Stacey
Good-Bye
THIS LITTLE ONE'S FOR YOU.
THE BAKERY MAKES A SPECIAL SUGARLESS CAKE.

THAT'S SO SWEET. NO PUN INTENDED.
SERIOUSLY. YOU THOUGHT OF EVERYTHING. I REALLY APPRECIATE IT.
LET'S EAT!

I WOULD NEVER, EVER FORGET THEM. AFTER ALL, I HAD ONE MURAL, TWENTY-EIGHT CARDS, AND THOUSANDS OF MEMORIES.

Good lick
Stasy. Have fun
in New Yurk.
-Margo Pike
Stacy
Goodbye
Stacey
I LOVE
love you
Stacey!!
Good-bye, Stacey.
I will always
miss you. I wish you
were my sister.
Love,
Charlotte

CHAPTER 12

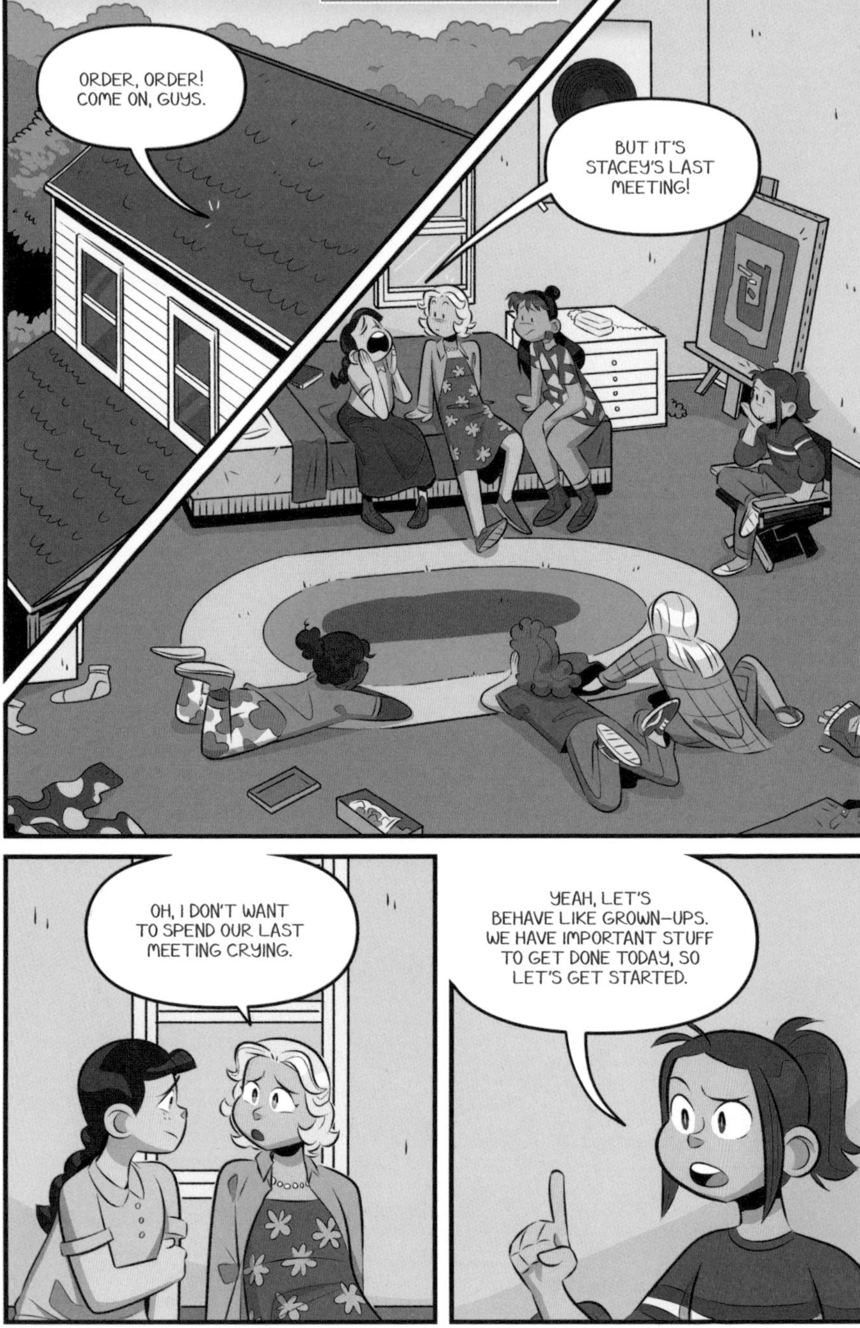

ORDER, ORDER! COME ON, GUYS.

BUT IT'S STACEY'S LAST MEETING!

AS WE ALL KNOW, STACEY IS LEAVING TOMORROW. WHEN SHE GOES, WE'LL NEED A NEW CLUB TREASURER.
SO IT'S TIME TO MAKE DAWN, FORMERLY OUR ALTERNATE OFFICER, THE TREASURER OF THE BABY-SITTERS CLUB.

CAN YOU COME STAND OVER HERE?
I WANT THIS TO BE OFFICIAL.

ANASTASIA ELIZABETH MCGILL. AS PRESIDENT OF THE BABY-SITTERS CLUB, I HEREBY THANK YOU FOR ALL YOUR HELP, FOR BEING RESPONSIBLE, AND FOR BEING OUR TREASURER.

YOU WERE OUR FIRST TREASURER AND A GOOD FRIEND. WE'LL REALLY MISS YOU.
OUR ALTERNATE OFFICER WILL TAKE OVER AS TREASURER.
DAWN READ SCHAFER, I HEREBY MAKE YOU TREASURER OF THE BABY-SITTERS CLUB.
YOU ARE NOW IN CHARGE OF THE TREASURY.
THANKS, KRISTY.

WITH THAT SETTLED, WE NEED TO FIGURE OUT HOW WE'LL COVER STACEY'S JOBS.

WELL, MAYBE WE CAN!
YEAH, I'M ALLOWED TO STAY OUT A LITTLE LATER THESE DAYS.

I THINK THAT'S A GOOD IDEA. YOU BOTH HAVE SHOWN YOURSELVES TO BE VERY RESPONSIBLE.

?
GREAT! I GUESS THERE'S JUST ONE LAST THING TO DO.

CHEERS!
TO STACEY!

TO STACEY!

CHAPTER 13

I COULDN'T REALLY SLEEP THAT NIGHT.

MORNING.

MORNING, HONEY.

SORRY, THE TOASTER'S ALREADY PACKED.

DO YOU WANT SOME CHEESE?

NO, THANKS.

I HATED THE
SIGHT OF MY
EMPTY ROOM.
Stacey

STACEY!
sniff!

HEY, STACEY!

OH MY GOSH!
See you soon, Stacey
gasp!
I'LL BE RIGHT DOWN!
OKAY!
squeeeaak

Need a baby-sitter?

Stacey McGill
14 W. 81st St., Apt. 12E
New York, NY
JK 5-8761

The New York Branch
of the Baby-sitters Club

I REALIZED I HADN'T GIVEN YOU MY NEW ADDRESS.
AND I'M NOT GOING TO FORGET THE BABY-SITTERS CLUB. IN FACT, IT'S GOING TO GROW.
THAT'S A GREAT IDEA!
AW!
STACEY, THE MOVERS ARE READY. TIME TO GO.
...HOW CAN I SAY GOOD-BYE TO YOU?

I'LL MISS YOU SO MUCH.

GOOD-BYE,
STACEY! GOOD-BYE!

Best Friends

Dear Stacey,

I bet this will keep you amuzed intil you get to NY. City. Maybe I will never have another best friend, but it would be wirth it. I mean it would be wirth it to have had you for my best freind even if it was for just a yer. You will always be my <u>best</u> best freind if you know what I mean. What I mean is I might get another best freind sometime but she wouldn't be as good a best freind as you.

AND YOU, CLAUDIA KISHI, WILL ALWAYS BE **MY** BEST FRIEND.

You are now leaving
Stoneybrook

I WAS READY FOR NEW YORK AND WHATEVER IT HELD FOR ME.

ANN M. MARTIN'S The Baby-sitters Club is one of the most popular series in the history of publishing — with more than 190 million books in print worldwide — and inspired a generation of young readers. Her novels include *Belle Teal, A Corner of the Universe* (a Newbery Honor book), *Here Today, A Dog's Life*, and *On Christmas Eve*, as well as the much-loved collaborations, *P.S. Longer Letter Later* and *Snail Mail No More*, with Paula Danziger, and *The Doll People* and *The Meanest Doll in the World*, written with Laura Godwin and illustrated by Brian Selznick. Ann lives in upstate New York.